50

Robbie and Ronnie

Robbie and Ronnie

By Christine Kliphuis

Illustrated by Charlotte Dematons

North-South Books

NEW YORK • LONDON

Copyright © 2002 by Nord-Süd Verlag AG, Gossau Zürich, Switzerland
First published in the Netherlands under the title *Robbie en Ronnie*
by De Vier Windstreken, Niederlande, an imprint of
Nord-Süd Verlag AG, Gossau Zürich, Switzerland.
English translation © 2002 by North-South Books Inc., New York

First published in the United States, Great Britain, Canada,
Australia, and New Zealand in 2002 by North-South Books,
an imprint of Nord-Süd Verlag AG, Gossau Zürich, Switzerland.

Distributed in the United States by North-South Books Inc., New York.

Library of Congress Cataloging-in-Publication Data is available.
A CIP catalogue record for this book is available from The British Library.
ISBN 0-7358-1626-3 (trade edition) 10 9 8 7 6 5 4 3 2 1
ISBN 0-7358-1627-1 (library edition) 10 9 8 7 6 5 4 3 2 1
Printed in Belgium

For more information about our books, and the authors and artists
who create them, visit our web site: www.northsouth.com

Robbie and Ronnie were best friends.

They lived next door to each other.
They were in the same class at school.

Robbie was chubby. Ronnie was thin.

They didn't care. They just liked each
other.

5

Every morning they walked to school
together.

"Hello, Jelly-Belly!" Ronnie would say.

"Hello, Bones!" Robbie would say.

They both would laugh.

Every Wednesday they went swimming
after school. One week when they got
to the pool they saw Dennis.

"Look who's here," said Robbie.

Dennis was a bully. He often picked on Robbie and Ronnie.

"Never mind," Ronnie said. "We're going to swim anyway."

"That's right," Robbie agreed.

Robbie wore a red swimming suit.

It was a bit tight.

Ronnie wore a yellow swimming suit.

It was a bit loose.

They jumped into the water.

"This is great!" said Robbie.

"Let's go on the slide," said Ronnie.

"Yes!" Robbie replied. "Come on."

They ran to the slide.

"No running!" shouted the lifeguard.

He always shouted that.

When they got to the slide, Dennis was there with his friends.

"Look, here are Fatso and Wimpy," he said with a nasty smile. He pointed at Robbie. "Look, guys, a real porker!"

His friends laughed.

Robbie didn't say anything. He looked sad.

"Leave him alone," Ronnie shouted. "You are a jerk!"

Dennis just laughed. "Do you want to fight, Wimpy?" he said. "I can knock you down with one punch!"

Ronnie didn't say anything. Now *he* looked sad.

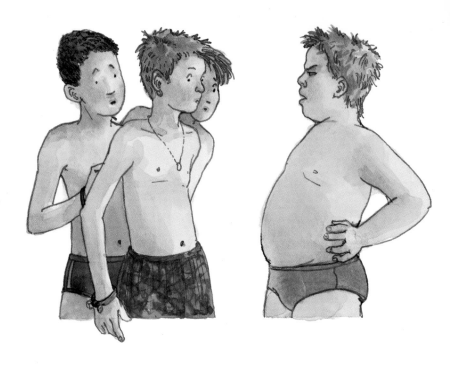

"Leave him alone," Robbie shouted. He stuck out his belly. "Do you know how much I weigh? If I sit on you, I'll flatten you!"

"Very flat," Ronnie agreed.

Robbie took a step forward. "Now, do you still want to fight?" he asked.

Dennis looked confused. "It was only a joke," he said. Then he and his friends walked off.

Robbie and Ronnie watched Dennis walk away.

"I guess he won't bother us anymore," said Robbie.

"He was really afraid of you," Ronnie said.

They laughed together, feeling proud and tough.

"Come on, let's go down the slide," said Ronnie.

They went down the slide three times— first on their stomachs, then on their backs, and then they slid down together.

It was a lot of fun.

"What should we do now?" Robbie asked.

"Let's swim underwater," Ronnie replied.

"Okay," said Robbie. "We can play ship-wreck."

"And I'll find a treasure!" said Ronnie.

They took deep breaths and swam to the bottom of the pool.

Ronnie kept his eyes shut. He searched the bottom with his hands. Suddenly, he felt something! He grabbed it and headed back up to the surface.

Ronnie couldn't believe his eyes. "Look, Robbie," he said. "I really did find a treasure!"

Robbie was amazed. "It's a necklace," he said. "And it's real gold!"

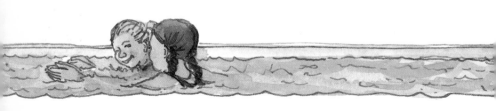

The necklace was engraved with a girl's name, Linda.

"Look, the clasp is broken," said Ronnie. "We'd better take it to the lifeguard. Maybe he'll know who owns it."

But when they got out of the water, Dennis and his friends were standing in front of them.

"What have you got there?" Dennis asked.

"Nothing," said Robbie.

"Nothing, zilch, zero," Ronnie added.

"I saw you looking at something," Dennis said. "Show it to me!"

Ronnie clasped the necklace tightly in his hand.

"Leave us alone," said Robbie, "or I'll sit on you, remember?"

"Is that so?" said Dennis.

He pushed Robbie. His friends joined in. They all pushed Robbie to the edge of the pool.

Suddenly, Robbie lost his balance. *Splash!* Into the pool he went! Dennis and his friends started laughing.

Robbie came up sputtering. He looked furious. "Ronnie!" he shouted. "Go and get the lifeguard! Hurry!"

Ronnie ran along the edge of the pool to
the lifeguard station.

"No running!" shouted the lifeguard.
"How many times do I have to tell you?"
he asked sternly.

Ronnie showed him the necklace. "I
found this," he said, panting. "And
Dennis tried to take it away."

He pointed at Dennis and his friends.

"Come here, you!" the lifeguard said. He
looked very angry.

Dennis and his friends quickly jumped
into the water and swam off.

"Oh, no you don't!" said the lifeguard. "Wait here," he told Ronnie. "I'll be right back."

He plunged into the water and raced after Dennis and his friends.

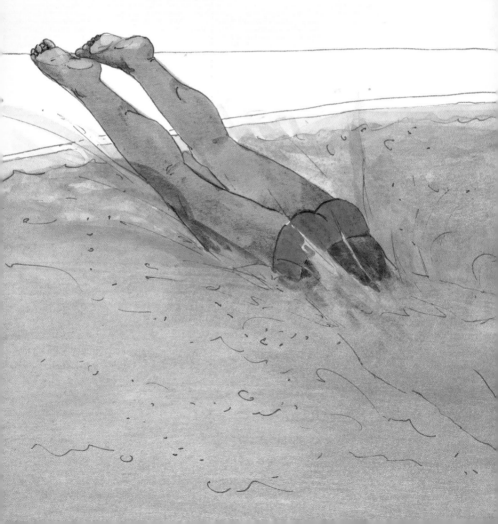

The lifeguard ordered the boys out of the water. "Get dressed and go home!"

Dennis and his friends walked away. They didn't look so tough anymore.

"Serves them right," said Robbie.

"Good riddance," said Ronnie.

"Did you give the necklace to the life-guard?" Robbie asked.

Ronnie shook his head. "I didn't get the chance."

The lifeguard walked over to Robbie and
Ronnie. "Well then, that's taken care of,"
he said and winked. "Now show me that
necklace."

Ronnie handed him the necklace. "Look,
it says Linda."

"Linda?" said the lifeguard.

He touched his neck. Then he looked at
the necklace. "This is mine!" he said. "I didn't
even know I'd lost it! Linda is my girl-
friend. She gave me this necklace. It's real
gold. Isn't it beautiful? You guys are great,"
he said, smiling. "Thanks!"

"You're welcome," said Ronnie. "But the
clasp is broken. That's why it fell off."

"I'll have to get it fixed," the lifeguard
said. "Thanks again!"

Robbie and Ronnie jumped back into the
pool. They were very happy. They'd found
a real treasure and dealt with Dennis and
his friends at the same time.

A little later, the lifeguard called out to them again. "Boys! Come with me." He took them to the office. The manager of the pool was there.

What could he want with them? They hadn't done anything wrong.

"I want to thank you," said the manager. "You found a necklace and returned it to its owner. You're honest, and I like that."

Robbie and Ronnie felt a little embarrassed.

"I think you deserve a reward," said the manager.

He gave them each a pen with the name of the pool written on it.

"Thank you, sir!" they said politely.

"And that's not all," the manager added. He took out a piece of paper and wrote:

Good for three free tickets each for the pool.

Then he signed his name at the bottom.

"Just show this at the ticket window," he said.

Robbie and Ronnie were delighted.

A pen with the name of the pool on it. Nobody in their class had that. And three free tickets for the pool!

"Thank you so much!" they said. Then they hurried off to get dressed.

On the way home Ronnie turned to Robbie. "We make a great team!" he said.

"We sure do!" replied Robbie. "Jelly-Belly and Bones forever!"

About the Author

Christine Kliphuis was born in Enschede, in the Netherlands, and now lives in The Hague. She majored in Slavic studies and now writes books full-time for children of all ages. This is her first book for North-South.

About the Artist

Charlotte Dematons was born in France and later moved to Amsterdam, where she studied book illustration at the Rietveld Academy and where she continues to live. This is her first book for North-South.

8/9/17 Stains Aubn
noted ↓ →